SOLEDAD SIGH-SIGHS
SOLEDAD SUSPIROS

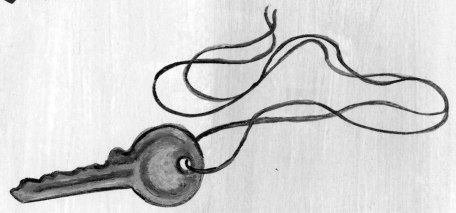

Story * Cuento
RIGOBERTO GONZÁLEZ

Illustrations * Ilustraciones
ROSA IBARRA

Children's Book Press * Editorial Libros para Niños
San Francisco, California

EVERY DAY, when Soledad gets home from school, the windows are as dark as cooked *gandules*. No one to talk to. Nothing fun to do.

Everyone in Soledad's apartment works. Papi at the grade school in the mornings and at the high school in the afternoons. Sweep-sweep. Mami at the laundry. Wash-dry-fold. Titi, Papi's sister, at the clothing store, where the price tag sensor sings, bleep-bleep!

Everything in Soledad's apartment also works. The lock when she turns the key in the door. The microwave, once she slides in the rice and beans her mother has left for her. The lights, so that, when everyone else arrives at night, they all know Soledad is safe. All is quiet. Soledad sigh-sighs.

TODOS LOS DÍAS cuando Soledad regresa de la escuela, las ventanas de su casa están más oscuras que los gandules cocidos. No hay con quien hablar. No hay nada divertido que hacer.

Todos en el apartamento de Soledad trabajan. Su papi trabaja en la escuela elemental por la mañana y por la tarde en la secundaria. Barre que te barre. Su mami en la lavandería. Lava-seca-dobla. Tití, la hermana de Papi, en el almacén de ropa donde los sensores de los precios suenan, ¡pip, pip!

Todas las cosas del apartamento trabajan también. La cerradura de la puerta, cuando Soledad le da vuelta con la llave. El microondas, cuando ella le pone adentro el arroz con habichuelas que le deja su mamá. Las luces que, cuando todos regresan por la noche, anuncian que Soledad está protegida. Todo está callado. Soledad suspira que te suspira.

"Knock-knock," says the neighbor, her knuckles at the door. "Are you home, Soledad?"

"Yes, Mrs. Ahmed," Soledad answers back.

"Very well, then," Mrs. Ahmed says. "I'll call your mother and let her know. Don't forget now . . . "

"Yes, I know," Soledad sigh-sighs. "Do my homework. Brush my teeth before I go to bed."

"Very well, then," Mrs. Ahmed says again.

Soledad says, "Thank you very much, Mrs. Ahmed."

—Tun-tún —la vecina toca con los nudillos en la puerta—. ¿Estás en casa, Soledad?

—Si, señora Ahmed —responde Soledad.

—Muy bien —dice la señora Ahmed—. Entonces llamaré a tu mamá para decirle que todo está bien. Y que no se te olvide...

—Sí, ya sé —Soledad suspira que te suspira—. Debo hacer la tarea de la escuela y lavarme los dientes antes de acostarme.

—Muy bien —repite la señora Ahmed. Soledad le dice: —Muchas gracias, señora Ahmed.

By the time everyone comes home, Soledad is asleep on the living room couch. Her math book lies at her side with a worksheet sandwiched between the pages like a slice of Swiss cheese. When Mami wakes her up it is already morning and time to wash-dry-dress to go to school. Papi and Titi wave at her from behind their cups of coffee.

Soledad sigh-sighs as she walks down the stoop, the key heavy around her neck.

"*Soledad Suspiros*," Mami calls out from the window. "Smile! You're going to see all your friends at school."

Soledad sighs again. If only she didn't have to be alone *after* school . . .

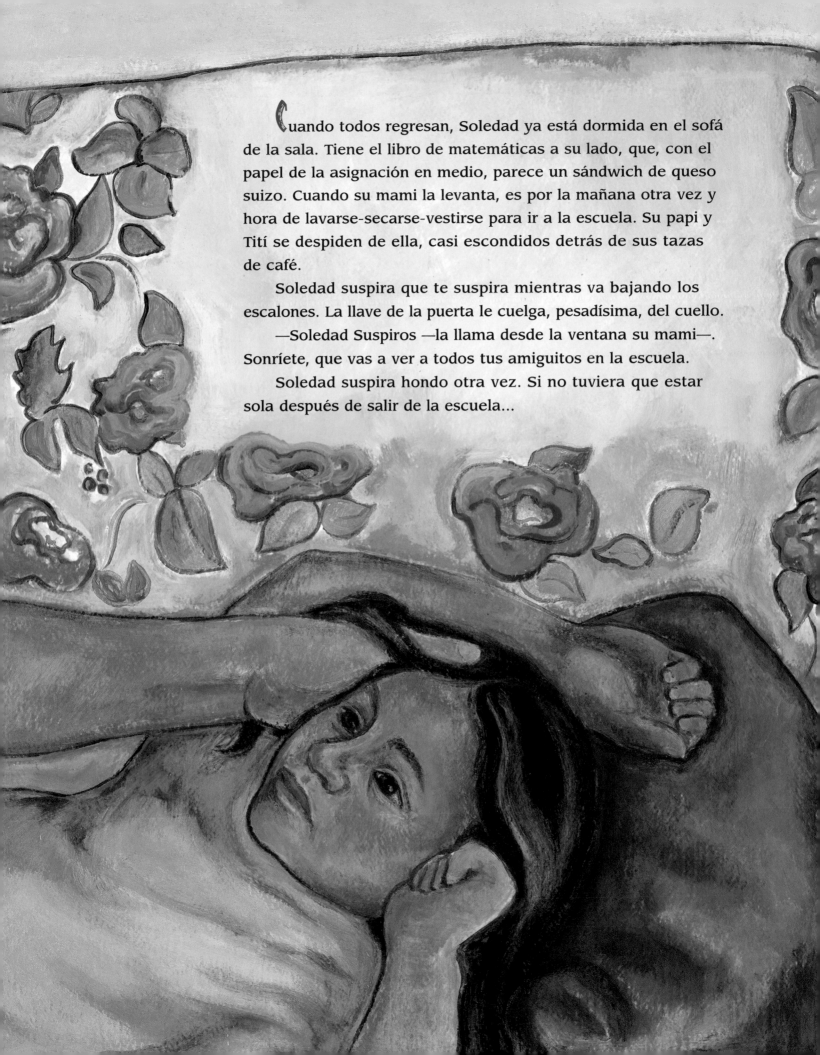

Cuando todos regresan, Soledad ya está dormida en el sofá de la sala. Tiene el libro de matemáticas a su lado, que, con el papel de la asignación en medio, parece un sándwich de queso suizo. Cuando su mami la levanta, es por la mañana otra vez y hora de lavarse-secarse-vestirse para ir a la escuela. Su papi y Tití se despiden de ella, casi escondidos detrás de sus tazas de café.

Soledad suspira que te suspira mientras va bajando los escalones. La llave de la puerta le cuelga, pesadísima, del cuello.

—Soledad Suspiros —la llama desde la ventana su mami—. Sonríete, que vas a ver a todos tus amiguitos en la escuela.

Soledad suspira hondo otra vez. Si no tuviera que estar sola después de salir de la escuela...

Soledad doesn't want to be by herself anymore. So she decides to have a little sister, just like Nedelsy. A little girl to *No-no* to and to *Sí-sí* to. She begins to practice.

"*No, no,* Felicidad," Soledad says out loud. "No more playing on the sidewalk. It's time for school."

"*Sí, sí,*" Soledad says. "We can play and eat *piraguas* in the afternoon."

Soledad ya se cansa de estar sola y decide que va a tener una hermanita como la de Nedelsy. Una niñita para decirle que no-no y que sí-sí. Lo practica:

—No, no, Felicidad —dice Soledad en voz alta—. Deja de jugar ya en la acera. Es hora de ir a la escuela.

—Sí, sí. Por la tarde podemos jugar y comer piraguas.

11

Going home again. Skipping this time because she's going to the playground with her little sister.

On the slide, Soledad goes first. And then she slides again, this time right behind Felicidad.

Soledad shows her sister how to jump in the sandbox, to climb up the jungle gym, and to kick an invisible ball so that it rises over the fence and lands on the other side of the street.

"Sorry, Mr. Wong," Soledad calls out to the *bodega* owner.

Mr. Wong waves back, looking confused.

De regreso a casa. Esta vez saltando y brincando porque va al parque con su hermanita.

En la chorrera, primero le toca a Soledad. Y se vuelve a deslizar, esta vez detrás de Felicidad.

Soledad le enseña a su hermanita a brincar en la caja de arena, a subirse a las barras del pasamanos y a patear una pelota invisible para que ésta suba bien alto, pase sobre la verja y termine al otro lado de la calle.

—Disculpe, señor Wong —Soledad le grita al dueño de la bodega. El señor Wong la saluda, bastante confundido.

13

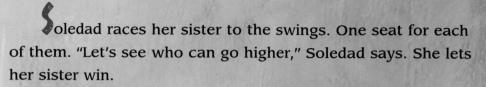

oledad races her sister to the swings. One seat for each of them. "Let's see who can go higher," Soledad says. She lets her sister win.

"*Sí, sí,* Felicidad," Soledad says. "You fly high, like a bird in the sky! Do you want to go home or do you want to play some more? Do you want to wear the key that opens the door?"

"Who are you talking to?"

Nedelsy and Jahniza stand next to the swings. Soledad slows down to a stop. Jahniza pushes the empty swing. Squeak-squeak, says the swing.

"Nobody," says Soledad.

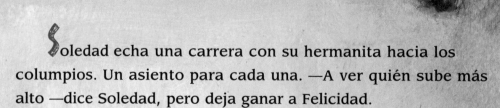

oledad echa una carrera con su hermanita hacia los columpios. Un asiento para cada una. —A ver quién sube más alto —dice Soledad, pero deja ganar a Felicidad.

—Sí, sí, Felicidad —dice Soledad—. ¡Vuelas tan alto que pareces un pájaro en el cielo! ¿Quieres que nos vayamos a casa o quieres jugar un rato más? ¿Quieres llevar la llave de la puerta?

—¿Con quién hablas? —Nedelsy y Jahniza están al lado de los columpios. Soledad va más despacio hasta detenerse. Jahniza empuja el columpio vacío. Scriich-scriich, rechina el columpio.

—Con nadie —dice Soledad.

14

"Silly girl," Jahniza says and giggles, hee-hee-hee.

"No, no," Nedelsy says. "It's not nice to make fun of people."

"I'm sorry, Soledad," Jahniza says.

"That's OK," Soledad sigh-sighs. "I was feeling lonely so I played pretend."

"Pretending what?" Jahniza asks.

Soledad sigh-sighs again. "I was pretending I had a little sister to be my friend."

Nedelsy says, "But we're your friends."

Soledad says, "Ohhh, not when I'm alone at home."

Jahniza leans over to whisper in Nedelsy's ear. Nedelsy nods her head. They each grab one of Soledad's hands and rush her out of the playground and up the stairs where Mrs. Ahmed waves hello.

"We'll call our grandma from your house, Soledad, and tell her where we are," Nedelsy says.

—¡Qué niña más loca! —dice Jahniza, y se ríe— ¡Ji, ji, ji!

—No, no —dice Nedelsy—. No es bueno burlarse de la gente.

—Lo siento, Soledad —se disculpa Jahniza.

—Está bien —suspira que te suspira Soledad—. Me sentía sola y me puse a jugar algo imaginario.

—¿Qué te imaginabas? —pregunta Jahniza.

Soledad suspira que te suspira otra vez: —Estaba jugando a que tenía una hermanita y que ella era mi amiga.

Nedelsy le contesta: —Pero si nosotras somos tus amigas.

Soledad le dice: —Hummm, pero no cuando estoy sola en mi casa.

Jahniza se acerca a Nedelsy y le susurra algo en el oído. Nedelsy le contesta que sí. Juntas toman a Soledad cada una de una mano y se la llevan corriendo del parque, suben los escalones, y allí las saluda la señora Ahmed.

—Vamos a llamar a Abuelita desde tu casa, Soledad, para decirle dónde estamos —dice Nedelsy.

17

The apartment doesn't look so big with people in it. Jahniza sits on the couch and begins to bounce.

"No, no, Jahniza," Nedelsy says. "We are guests."

"I know," Jahniza sigh-sighs. She sounds like Soledad.

"Are these all your books?" Nedelsy asks.

"Here are some more," Soledad replies.

"Reading is something you can do when you're alone," Nedelsy says in her schoolteacher voice.

"I only like to read out loud to Mami," Jahniza says, flipping through the pages of a picture book.

"I have to do everything by myself," says Soledad. "Like finish my homework and listen to music and heat my dinner."

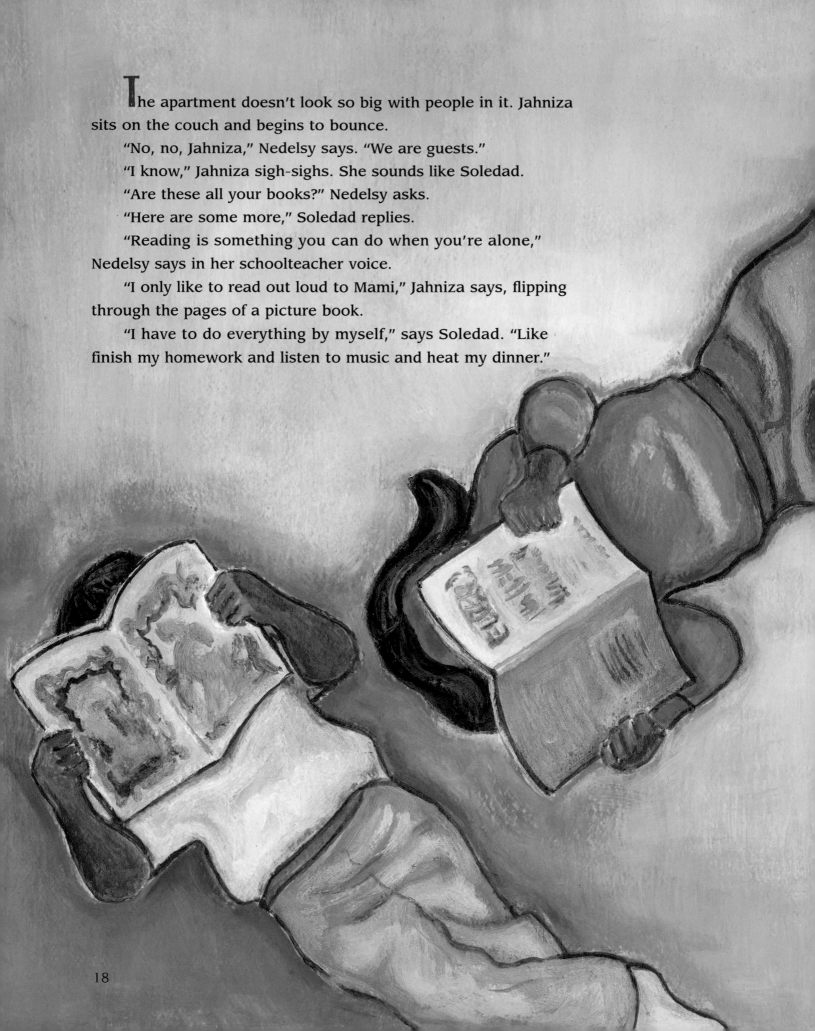

El apartamento, cuando hay gente, no se ve tan grande.
Jahniza se sienta en el sofá y empieza a brincar.

—Jahniza, no, no —le dice Nedelsy—. Acuérdate que
estamos de visita.

—Sí, ya lo sé —Jahniza suspira que te suspira. Suena
igualito como Soledad.

—Todos estos libros, ¿son tuyos? —pregunta Nedelsy.

—Y aquí tengo más —le contesta Soledad.

—Leer es una de las cosas que uno puede hacer cuando
está solo —dice Nedelsy en su tono de maestra de escuela.

—A mí sólo me gusta leerle en voz alta a mi mami —dice
Jahniza, pasando rápidamente las páginas de un libro ilustrado.

—A mí me toca hacerlo todo solita —dice Soledad—:
terminar la asignación, escuchar música y calentar la comida.

"But playing music by yourself can be fun," Nedelsy says. "My house is so busy, there are times I'd love to listen to music all by myself."

"Sometimes," says Soledad. "But listening with someone else is even better." She walks over to the radio and turns it on.

Jahniza shakes her hips. "Who wants to dance the *mambo*?"

"*Merengue!*" says Soledad. She shakes her hips even faster. The girls giggle.

Nedelsy dances around the room. "But there's so much more to do here on your own. You can wrap sandwiches for your Papi's lunch, you can write a letter or put things in the living room in order." She begins to neaten up some magazines.

"That's true," Soledad says. "But sometimes I just like to look out the window and watch for animal shapes in the clouds."

Nedelsy's eyes light up. She says, "I like that, too!"

—Pero puedes gozar escuchando música cuando estás sola —dice Nedelsy—. Mi casa siempre está tan y tan ocupada, que a veces quisiera poder escuchar música yo sola.

—A veces, sí —dice Soledad—. Pero escuchar con alguien es mejor. —Camina hacia el radio y lo prende.

Jahniza mueve las caderas. —¿Quién quiere bailar mambo?

—¡Merengue! —dice Soledad. Remenea las caderas bien ligero. Las niñas se ríen.

Nedelsy baila alrededor de la sala. —Hay muchísimas cosas que puedes hacer tú sola. Puedes envolverle los *sandwiches* del almuerzo a tu papá, puedes ponerte a escribir una carta o a poner en orden la sala. —Nedelsy empieza a arreglar algunas revistas.

—Es verdad —dice Soledad—. Pero a veces me gusta más mirar por la ventana y observar los animales que forman las nubes.

A Nedelsy le brillan los ojos. —¡A mí también me gusta hacer eso! —dice.

"I see an elephant!" Jahniza points it out. The other girls run to the window.

"So do I!" Soledad shouts.

"How about that one over there?" Nedelsy says.

"A shoe?" Jahniza says. "What color?" Nedelsy asks.

"A rainbow-colored shoe," replies Soledad. "To skip over the skyscrapers, two by two!"

"Look at that cloud over there," says Janhiza. "It looks like a *bizcocho*!"

"What flavor?" Nedelsy asks.

"A rainbow-flavored *bizcocho*," says Jahniza. "It tastes like strawberry, *chinas,* and pineapples."

"*Sí, sí,* Jahniza," says Nedelsy. "Very good."

"That one reminds me of an island," Soledad says.

"Hawaii?" Jahniza asks.

"Puerto Rico!" the other girls shout.

—Veo un elefante —dice Jahniza y lo señala. Las otras dos niñas corren hacia la ventana.

—¡Y yo también! —grita Soledad.

—¿Qué les parece aquélla que está allá? —pregunta Nedelsy.

—¿Un zapato? —contesta Jahniza.

—¿De qué color? —vuelve a preguntar Nedelsy.

—¡Es un zapato pintado de arco iris, para saltar de dos en dos los rascacielos! —responde Soledad.

—Miren aquella nube —dice Jahniza—. Ésa parece un bizcocho.

—¿De qué sabor? —pregunta Nedelsy.

—Un bizcocho con sabor de arco iris —dice Jahniza—. Sabe a fresa, a china y a piña.

—Sí, Jahniza, sí —dice Nedelsy—. Muy bien.

—Aquélla a mí me hace pensar en una isla —dice Soledad.

—¿Hawai? —le pregunta Jahniza.

—¡Puerto Rico! —gritan las otras niñas.

"Let's do something else now. Does the TV work?" Jahniza asks, holding the remote in her hand.

"It just broke yesterday." Soledad sigh-sighs.

"Even better! It's bad for your eyes." Nedelsy sounds like a teacher again.

"Oh, look, Jahniza," Nedelsy says. "A treasure box!"

"*Sí, sí,* Nedelsy," Jahniza grins. "Now the fun really begins."

Soledad places her finger on her chin. Why didn't she see that crate there before?

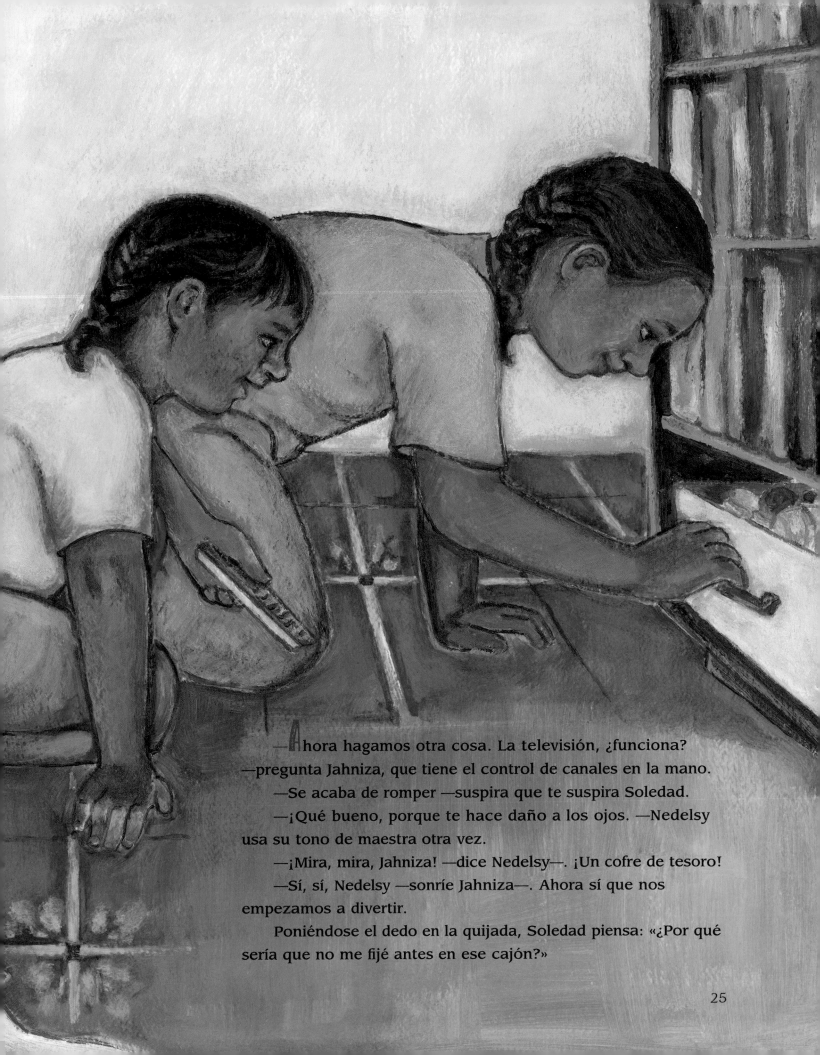

—Ahora hagamos otra cosa. La televisión, ¿funciona?
—pregunta Jahniza, que tiene el control de canales en la mano.

—Se acaba de romper —suspira que te suspira Soledad.

—¡Qué bueno, porque te hace daño a los ojos. —Nedelsy
usa su tono de maestra otra vez.

—¡Mira, mira, Jahniza! —dice Nedelsy—. ¡Un cofre de tesoro!

—Sí, sí, Nedelsy —sonríe Jahniza—. Ahora sí que nos
empezamos a divertir.

Poniéndose el dedo en la quijada, Soledad piensa: «¿Por qué
sería que no me fijé antes en ese cajón?»

25

Nedelsy fishes out a deck of cards, more books, a photo album, crayons, old hats and scarves, a spool of red ribbon, construction paper, glue, and a watercolor set her teacher gave Soledad on the final day of summer school.

"Here," Nedelsy says, holding the ribbon in her hand. "Let me teach you how to braid your hair like ours. It's tricky to do that by yourself, but it's easy when somebody helps you."

After awhile, Jahniza jumps up off the floor. "Guess what I drew!" Jahniza says, holding up a piece of paper.

"*Qué bonita bandera, qué bonita bandera,*" Nedelsy sings.

"I want to draw a flower for Brooklyn," Soledad says, touching her new braids.

"Why only one?" Jahniza says. "Let's draw a million!"

"Then we'd better start now," Nedelsy says. The girls laugh.

Nedelsy saca unas barajas, más libros, un álbum de fotos, crayones, unas bufandas y unos sombreros viejos, un rollo de cinta roja, papel de construcción, pega y una caja de acuarelas que la maestra le regaló a Soledad el último día de clases de verano.

—Mira —dice Nedelsy, que tiene la cinta en la mano—. Déjame enseñarte a trenzarte el pelo como el de nosotras. Es un poco difícil hacerlo una sola, pero es fácil cuando otra persona te ayuda.

Al ratito, Jahniza se levanta de un brinco. —¡A que no adivinan lo que dibujé! —dice y les enseña su hoja de papel a las otras.

—¡Qué bonita bandera, qué bonita bandera! —canta Nedelsy.

—Yo quiero dibujar una flor para Brooklyn —dice Soledad, tocándose las nuevas trenzas.

—¿Por qué sólo una? —responde Jahniza—. ¿Por qué no dibujamos un millón?

—Entonces mejor empezemos ahora mismo —dice Nedelsy. Las tres se ponen a reír.

"You know what, Soledad?" Nedelsy asks. "I think you're pretty lucky, having fun with your friends sometimes and being on your own at others."

"Can I still play pretend?" Soledad asks shyly.

"*Sí, sí*, Soledad. Of course you can," Nedelsy says. "As long as you don't forget about your other friends."

"We're more like sisters now," Jahniza says. "Since we wear the same braids."

They shake their heads to make their braids bounce like three pairs of wings flapping in the wind.

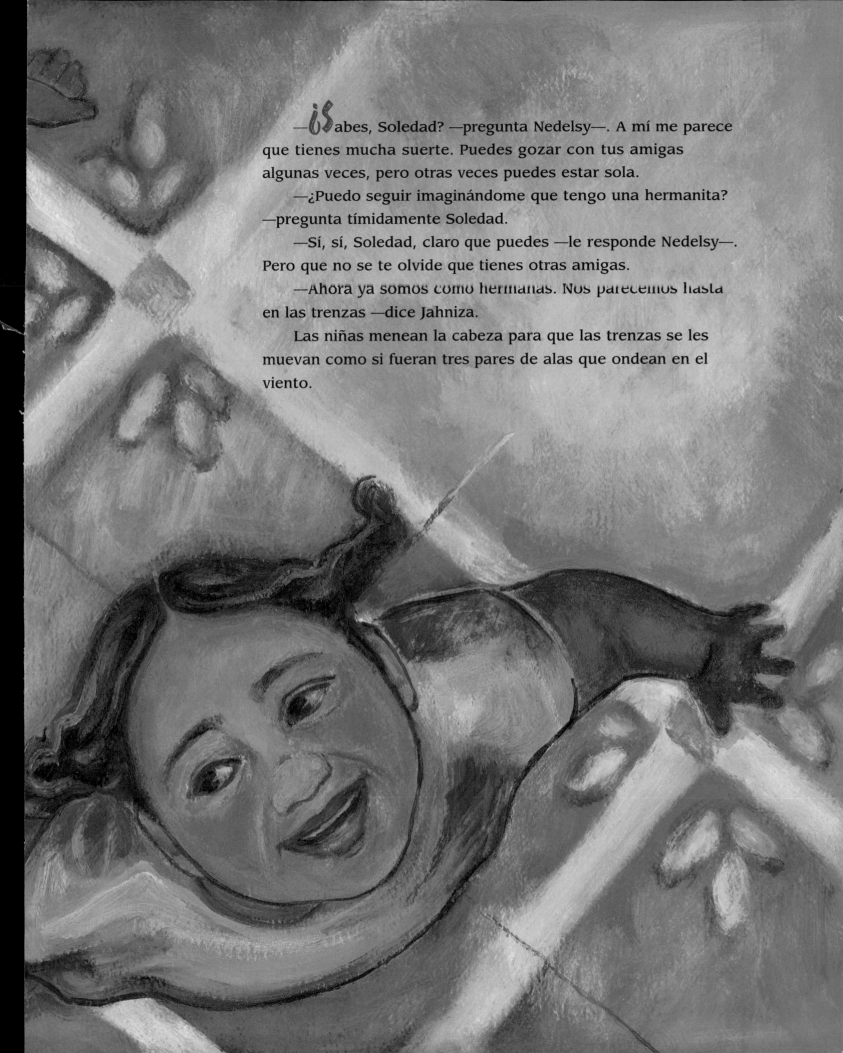

—¿Sabes, Soledad? —pregunta Nedelsy—. A mí me parece que tienes mucha suerte. Puedes gozar con tus amigas algunas veces, pero otras veces puedes estar sola.

—¿Puedo seguir imaginándome que tengo una hermanita? —pregunta tímidamente Soledad.

—Sí, sí, Soledad, claro que puedes —le responde Nedelsy—. Pero que no se te olvide que tienes otras amigas.

—Ahora ya somos como hermanas. Nos parecemos hasta en las trenzas —dice Jahniza.

Las niñas menean la cabeza para que las trenzas se les muevan como si fueran tres pares de alas que ondean en el viento.

Jahniza yawns and asks, "Is it time to go?"

A little bit tired, Soledad sigh-sighs, "I guess it's time for me to be alone again."

"Yeah," says Nedelsy. "Can I come over and play with you when it's too crazy at my house?"

"Yes," Soledad says, "and we can be alone together."

"And that way you only have to be all alone a little bit at a time," Nedelsy adds.

"Until your *mami* gets home!" Jahniza says, pointing at the door.

"Mami, you're early!" Soledad shouts. She runs to the door and gives her mother a big kiss on the cheek.

Mami asks, "Soledad Suspiros, what did you do today?"

"So many things, Mami," Soledad sigh-sighs, but in a happy way.

Jahniza bosteza y pregunta: —¿Ya es hora de irnos?

Un poco cansada, Soledad suspira que te suspira: —Parece que ya llegó la hora de volver a estar sola.

—Sí —dice Nedelsy—. ¿Me dejas volver a venir a jugar contigo cuando no aguante el alboroto de mi casa?

—Claro —responde Soledad— y así podremos estar solas, pero juntas.

—Y así sólo tienes que estar solita por ratos —agrega Nedelsy.

—¡Hasta que llegue a casa tu mami! —dice Jahniza, señalando la puerta.

—¡Mami está aquí! —exclama Soledad. Corre a la puerta y le da un beso muy grande en la mejilla a su mamá, que acaba de llegar.

Mami le dice: —Cuéntame lo que hiciste hoy, Soledad Suspiros.

—Tantas y tantas cosas, mami —responde Soledad, suspira que te suspira, pero esta vez de felicidad.

THIS BOOK *is dedicated to all of the after-school programs across the country, to the artists and teachers who guide children into the world of creativity, and to the children who keep their senses open to the possibility of magic. And to my niece, my song and dance, Halima.* —R.G.

RIGOBERTO GONZÁLEZ was born in Bakersfield, California, and raised in Michoacán, Mexico. The son and grandson of migrant farm workers, he is an award-winning writer of poetry and fiction. Since completing his third university degree, he has worked mostly in New York and primarily with children and young adults as a literacy specialist and creative writing teacher.

Rosa's son Gabriel poses for the painting on page 2.

FROM THE AUTHOR . . .

During the two years I taught in an after-school program, the children from the primarily Puerto Rican and Dominican community inspired me with their wonderful stories, poems and drawings. Together, we confronted a social reality: that many parents work long hours; that there are very few such places where children can explore, dream, and create; and that there are more children than available slots in good programs. This story is about a little girl who has not yet been served by an after-school program. There are many more children like her. But I suspect that, like Soledad, they are also survivors and will employ their creative instincts in their own special ways. I wrote about Soledad because I too was a latchkey kid and I know about feeling lonely. This book is a small gift for the children who can use a little help discovering what already breathes inside of them: talent and imagination.

—Rigoberto González

I DEDICATE *this book to my father who taught me what family love is, and to the children I adore: my Klara, Nina, Kristina, and Gabriel*—R.I.

ROSA IBARRA is a painter whose work is exhibited and collected internationally. Born and raised in Puerto Rico and schooled in Paris and at the University of Massachusetts, Amherst, she went on to apprentice in Paris with her father, the painter, Alfonso Arana.

Story copyright © 2003 by Rigoberto González
Illustrations copyright © 2003 by Rosa Ibarra

Editors: Ina Cumpiano and Dana Goldberg
Spanish translator: Jorge Argueta
Spanish native reader: Laura Chastain
Puerto Rican reviewer: Marisela Laborde
Art Direction, design and production: Aileen Friedman

Our thanks to: William Cumpiano, Jim Ault, Bob Marshall, Mario César Romero, Diógenes Ballester, Zhane and Shanya Rivera, Margarita Jimenez, Carmen and Graciano Vásquez-Matos, Noél Torres, Luisa Alvarado-Tull, Yarisa Torres, Sylvia Reyes, Yoko Esaki, and Jenny Sienkiewicz, Carlota Maldonado, and the staff of Children's Book Press.

Photo of Rigoberto by Gary Suson; photo of Rosa by William Cumpiano.

Children's Book Press is a nonprofit publisher of multicultural literature for children, supported in part by grants from the California Arts Council. Write us for a complimentary catalog: Children's Book Press, 2211 Mission Street, San Francisco, CA 94110; (415) 821-3080.

Visit our website at www.childrensbookpress.org

Library of Congress Cataloging-in-Publication Data
González, Rigoberto.
Soledad sigh-sighs / story, Rigoberto González ; illustrations, Rosa Ibarra ; translation, Jorge Argueta = Soledad suspiros / cuento, Rigoberto
González ; ilustraciones, Rosa Ibarra ; traducción, Jorge Argueta.
p. cm.
Summary: Soledad's friends help her discover the many things that she can do to entertain herself while she is alone in her apartment.
ISBN 0-89239-180-4
[1. Loneliness—Fictoin. 2. Imagination—Fiction. 3. Apartment houses—Fiction. 4. Hispanic Americans—Fiction. 5. Spanish language materials—Bilingual.] I. Title: Soledad suspiros. II. Ibarra, Rosa, ill. III. Title.
PZ73 .G592 2003   [E]—dc21
                                2002067721

Printed in Singapore by Tien Wah Press.

10 9 8 7 6 5 4 3 2

Distributed to the book trade by Publishers Group West. Quantity discounts are available through the publisher for educational and nonprofit use.